ASK EINSTEIN!

ALAN TRUSSELL-CULLEN

illustrated by
Lorenzo Van Der Lingen

LEARNING MEDIA®

Haskell School

Distributed in the United States of America by Pacific Learning,
P.O. Box 2723, Huntington Beach, CA 92647-0723
Web site: www.pacificlearning.com

Published 1999 by Learning Media Limited,
Box 3293, Wellington 6001, New Zealand
Web site: www.learningmedia.com

10 9 8 7 6 5 4 3

Printed in Hong Kong

ISBN 0 478 22919 4

PL 9150

Henry
1125 Maple Lane
Weatherly

November 19

Miss Wilson
Room 9
Weatherly Elementary School
Mornington Road
Weatherly 28470

Dear Miss Wilson

About my homework ...
I know we had to write a letter to someone,
and I did start to write to Uncle Tyson.
But, as you can see, this letter is written to
you. I've even drawn some pictures.

I didn't finish the letter to Uncle Tyson, but it isn't my fault. It really isn't, Miss Wilson. Ask Einstein!

Einstein is our cat.

Magnifying glass needed to see "peanut" brain.

We call him Einstein because he isn't.
Isn't bright, that is.
It's meant as a kind of joke.
You see, Einstein was a very famous
scientist. He was very bright. Get it?

IQ = 989,752,975,674,567   IQ = $2\frac{1}{2}$

(Well, we all thought it was funny!)

If the real Einstein's IQ was, say,
989, 752, 975, 674, 567, then our Einstein's
IQ would be two and a half (on a good day).

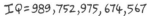

Footnote: Your IQ is meant to show how brainy you are.

Anyway, our Einstein isn't exactly brilliant. In fact, most of the time he's just plain stupid!

This is Einstein watching TV.

This is Einstein appearing on TV!

This is Einstein hiding from the birds.

This is Einstein doing some really hard thinking.

Of course, we love him all the same.

Except when he does stupid things,
which is most of the time!

What sort of stupid things?
Well, like the things he sits on.

Cats are supposed to sit on mats and things like that, right?

NOT OUR CAT!

He likes to sit on things that move.

Like my skateboard!

He often climbs onto it when it's on my bedroom floor. He just curls up like it's the most ordinary thing a cat can do.

Sometimes he even goes to sleep on it. That was fine until yesterday afternoon. Instead of leaving my skateboard in the bedroom, I left it by the back steps.

That didn't bother Einstein. He climbed on anyway. The trouble was ...
... the path is on a slope. When Einstein climbed on, the skateboard started to roll.

Now, a smart cat would have jumped off. A dumb cat would have at least fallen off.

But not Einstein!

He was going to take the full ride, wherever that went.

That "full ride" was right down the side of the house.

The only problem was ...
... Mom happened to be up a ladder there.

She was painting the house.

She was slapping on paint with her brush
and thinking her own thoughts.

Now, Einstein can't even ride a bike,
let alone a crazy skateboard on the loose.

But somehow that cat just happened to steer
that skateboard right under Mom's ladder.
This gave Mom a granddaddy of a fright.

That's why she dropped the paint can. It's also why she said words that she tells me I'm not allowed to say.

The paint was blue!

Einstein found out that it was blue paint.
He couldn't help but find out – most of it
landed on top of him.

He got a fright too.
That was why he jumped off the skateboard
and ran back up the steps.

He happened to rush by my grandpa, who was going out for his afternoon stroll.

Grandpa has a stroll every afternoon at exactly four o'clock. You can set your watch by Grandpa.

"Was that a blue streak?" asked Grandpa.
Mom didn't answer. She was too mad
about the paint.

"Going to paint the path the same color as
the house?" he asked.

Mom glared at him.

Meanwhile, Dad was coming up the path reading the paper.

That was when he found my skateboard.

I knew he'd found my skateboard because I saw him pass my window.

← Me, working very hard on my homework.

He was going faster than I'd ever seen anyone travel on a skateboard.

Until he crashed into the mailbox!

Grandpa heard the crash. "Expecting a letter?" he called out. Then he chuckled to himself.

Now, to get back to Einstein (who by this time was a lovely shade of blue).
He shot into the house, straight down the hall, and into my room.

That's where I was doing my homework, honest I was, Miss Wilson. So what does Einstein do? He leaps up on the desk and leaves his painty pawprints all over my desk and my homework.

That's why I couldn't finish the letter to Uncle Tyson. It really is.

Honest. Ask Einstein!

By the way, it was water-based paint, so we managed to wash it out of Einstein's fur – after we'd caught him!

Extra thick gardening gloves

We used the hose to wash him down. He struggled so much that we got paint all over ourselves and the yard.

Dad kept saying, "Let me do the squirting!
Let me do the squirting!
The stupid cat!"

Then he said, "Give me the hose now!"

So I did!

When we'd changed our clothes, we put
Einstein in the car and took him to the vet
for a checkup, just in case.
The vet thought it was very funny.

Then we took Dad to the doctor to check
that he hadn't broken anything. Turned out
that all Dad had broken was the mailbox.
And doctors don't fix mailboxes, do they?

After going to the doctor's, we went to the hardware store to buy a new mailbox. I said we should get a super-strong one so that it wouldn't break the next time Dad crashed into it.

Dad said there wasn't going to be a next time. My skateboard was going to be kept somewhere safe – away from our pea-brained cat!

Then we took Mom to the store to buy some more blue paint. The storekeeper looked puzzled. "You've used a lot of paint," he said.

Dad wanted to tell him about it, but Mom just gave him one of those looks that mean "Don't you dare!"
Dad just smiled and gave a sort of snort. Mom heard him, and you could see she wasn't pleased. She went to stand on his foot. Only she stood on the storekeeper's foot instead!

So, Miss Wilson, that's the end of the story, really ... and why I'm writing to you instead of to Uncle Tyson.

It really is! Truly!

Honestly!

Ask Einstein!
And, anyway, with so much going on in our house, it's a wonder I managed to do any homework at all!

Henry